Jacob and the Bee Man

PRAISE FOR *STORYSHARES*

"One of the brightest innovators and game-changers in the education industry."
– Forbes

"Your success in applying research-validated practices to promote literacy serves as a valuable model for other organizations seeking to create evidence-based literacy programs."
- Library of Congress

"We need powerful social and educational innovation, and Storyshares is breaking new ground. The organization addresses critical problems facing our students and teachers. I am excited about the strategies it brings to the collective work of making sure every student has an equal chance in life."
– Teach For America

"Around the world, this is one of the up-and-coming trailblazers changing the landscape of literacy and education."
- International Literacy Association

"It's the perfect idea. There's really nothing like this. I mean wow, this will be a wonderful experience for young people."   - Andrea Davis Pinkney, Executive Director, Scholastic

"Reading for meaning opens opportunities for a lifetime of learning. Providing emerging readers with engaging texts that are designed to offer both challenges and support for each individual will improve their lives for years to come. Storyshares is a wonderful start."
- David Rose, Co-founder of CAST & UDL

Jacob and the Bee Man

Kelly Winters

STORYSHARES

Story Share, Inc.
New York. Boston. Philadelphia

Storyshares
Story Share, Inc.
24 N. Bryn Mawr Avenue #340
Bryn Mawr, PA 19010-3304
www.storyshares.org

Inspiring reading with a new kind of book.

Interest Level: High School
Grade Level Equivalent: 1.8

9781973365334

Book design by Storyshares

Printed in the United States of America

Storyshares Presents

1

Last year, I did something stupid. I'm not going to tell you what it was, just that it was stupid. It was also against the law. I never did it again, and I was lucky the police didn't come after me for it. But that doesn't mean I'm not still stupid sometimes.

Like the day I threw a chunk of cement and smashed the Bee Man's hive.

I was having a terrible day. I had gone all over town on my bike, looking for a summer job. There were no jobs. The mill closed last year. Most of the people in town had worked there. When it closed, all the adults who used to work there took all the jobs that teenagers used to do. Mowing lawns, delivering papers, taking care of pets. Fast food jobs, cashier jobs. Every job.

And the jobs that weren't taken by adults were going to be filled by the other kids. Not me.

The owner at the car wash folded his arms, gave me a mean stare, and told me, "I don't hire kids like you."

Great. So I rode around all that hot morning just wanting to punch myself in the head for doing that stupid thing. *Would people ever forget it? Not likely.*

I was riding my bike down the street behind ours, past the Bee Man's house. The road there is broken and bumpy. Maybe it never gets fixed because the road crews are afraid of his bees.

The Bee Man is this weird old guy.

He has about a hundred beehives in his yard. They look like wooden boxes piled on top of each other. Millions — maybe billions! — of bees live in them.

He wears a big hat and baggy old clothes. No one has ever seen his face. He covers it with a veil to keep out the bees. He carries a little metal thing that looks like a teapot. Smoke comes out of it and he puffs the smoke over the bees. I have no idea why he does that. It's just part of his weirdness. You can hear him humming, and the bees humming, from down the block.

I was riding my bike past his house and WHAM! a yellow and black bug zoomed out and stung me on the leg. I saw it! It moved over and stung me again. And again!

I was already mad about the jobs, but this was just too much. I was as mad as a bee myself. I jumped off my bike and threw it down. I yelled. I swore. I grabbed a huge chunk of broken road and threw it over his fence. Right at a box full of bees.

Smash! The beehive fell to the ground.

Bees came boiling out! I jumped on my bike and rode away as fast as I could. My leg was killing me! It felt like it was on fire!

Mrs. Biel came out of her house on the other side of the road and yelled, "Jacob Brown, I saw you! I'm telling your mother what you did! You belong in jail after what you did last year! And now this! You'll be sorry!"

Oh great, I thought. *What if she called the cops?*

Another stupid thing!

2

I got home and went inside. My leg was puffing up. It was already bigger than my other leg. It hurt like crazy.

There was a note on the kitchen table.

Hi Jacob,

There is lunch in the refrigerator. I got a call from the donut shop. They want me to come in tonight and work until they close at 9. You can make your own supper.

I love you,

Mom

My mom was not stupid. She had never done anything against the law. She had two jobs. Answering phones at the dentist's office during the day was one. Then there was working at the donut shop at night.

The morning of the Big Hive Smash-Up, she told me that I better find a job for the summer. We were running out of money.

Ever since my dad died last year, our money has gotten tighter and tighter. Now, Mrs. Biel would probably call my mom at the donut shop and tell her what I did. Right before she called the cops.

Great.

I looked in the refrigerator. There was some bread and some baloney. A couple of apples. Some milk. And that was about it. I made a sandwich with one piece of bread and one piece of baloney. That was so there would be enough left for my Mom.

I spent the rest of the day lying on the couch with my leg killing me. We didn't have TV. Or internet. Cable cost too much money. And I'm not much of a reader. I called some of my friends, but none of them answered.

It was probably the longest day of my life.

That night my Mom came home at 9:30. She opened my door. I pretended to be asleep. A crack of light hit me right in the eye.

"Jacob?" she said. Her voice was sharp. "Wake up. I need to talk to you."

I rubbed my eyes. I could tell she knew I was really awake. There was no point in faking it. I sat up.

She came in and sat down. She smelled like sugar donuts.

"Jacob. Mrs. Biel told me you broke one of Cliff Finley's beehives. What did you do that for?"

"Finley? Who is Cliff Finley?" I asked.

"You know who he is. I called him and talked to him. Do you know how much that beehive cost?"

"How much?"

She sighed. "I have no idea. But whatever it is, I can't pay for it. He says you can work for him until it's paid for. You're going over there at nine tomorrow morning."

"I can't work for him! He's crazy! He'll kill me! He'll make all his bees sting me!"

"If you don't go, he'll call the police. You can't afford to get in trouble again. If you get a police record with your bad grades in school, you'll never get a job."

3

The next morning at nine o'clock, I was on his doorstep. My leg was still hurting so much that I couldn't walk straight. But I went.

I knocked, but no one answered. I hoped he wasn't home. All around me, bees were buzzing and tickling flowers. I tried to stand as still as I could. I hoped they wouldn't notice me.

Did they know I was the one who broke their hive?

I went around back. There he was. He was taking apart a beehive and looking at the bees. I couldn't see his face behind his veil. *Had anyone ever seen his face?* Maybe he was born with those bee clothes on. Maybe even his mother had never seen his face.

He turned around and looked at me. "I don't know why you wrecked my hive and I don't care," he said. "The hedge clippers are in that shed over there. See the hedge that goes along the side of my yard? Start trimming it. Exactly four feet high, straight across." He chopped his arm out sideways to show me. He handed me a long stick. "Exactly as high as this stick. And you'll keep doing it until you do it right. So no screwing around."

I got the clippers and got to work. It was hot. After a while I got big blisters on both hands, but I didn't say anything. I tried wrapping my hand in the end of my shirt. It helped a little.

The Bee Man went around his yard. He opened the top of each pile of hive boxes. He puffed smoke into it. He lifted the lid and peeked inside. Blew more smoke. Then he took out wooden rectangles. They looked like picture frames, but they were covered with bees.

He did all this bare-handed! No gloves at all. Wow. I kept waiting for the bees to sting him, but they never did. Even though his hands were right there. Maybe they knew who he was. Maybe they were afraid to sting him!

Hours went by. The sun moved slowly across the sky. It got hotter and hotter. I clipped all the way around the yard. The hedge looked great.

I didn't look great and I didn't feel great. My leg was puffed up even bigger now. I felt hot all over, inside and out. I felt sick.

Finally, I finished.

"OK, I'm done," I said.

He looked at the hedge a long time. "Good," he said. "I will see you tomorrow, exactly at nine."

I said, "Tomorrow? But I'm done! I worked all day!"

He laughed. "No, you're not. Not at all. Do you know how much a hive full of bees and honey costs? You'll be back tomorrow. You'll be back until I say you're done."

4

"Mom," I said that night, "this guy is working me too hard. How do I know when I'm done working for him? What if he never says I'm done?"

"Oh, I'm sure he'll tell you."

"But he won't! He's going to make me work for him all summer!"

"Good. You need something to keep you busy. If you're busy, maybe you won't have time to break other people's things."

"Mom!"

"I mean it, Jacob. We can't afford to pay for that broken hive. We can barely afford to pay for our house. You're lucky he's not calling the police. You're lucky no one called them last year. You need to straighten yourself out."

I groaned. When I'm 40 and old, people will probably still be telling me, "After all those bad things you did, back when you were a kid..."

5

So, I started my summer of servanthood to the Bee Man.

The next day, I saw his face. He had his hat off when I got there. He was just a regular old guy. Dark eyes, white hair. Lined face. But he was wide and strong. Not someone you would mess with.

"Tomorrow is garbage day," he said. "Carry those cans of trash to the curb. Next, get the hive you broke and put it out with the trash."

I went over to the hive. He had taken the bees out. Or maybe they all flew away. Now there was just a pile of banged-up wooden boxes. I felt terrible. It was a stupid thing to do.

I carried them out to the curb and put them gently on top of the cans. But it was too late to be gentle, now.

I spent the rest of the day weeding his flower gardens. Sweat poured down my face. Bees buzzed and flew around me. None of them stung me.

Sometimes I stopped weeding and watched them. They put their heads deep into every flower. Their bodies were covered with golden hairs. Yellow dust from the flowers stuck to all the hairs.

They moved quickly. It was like they hated to waste any time. I was surprised. I had never looked at a bee before. They were kind of interesting to watch.

Late in the afternoon, I looked up. The Bee Man was watching me. I'd been so busy looking at the bees that I had forgotten to weed.

"Uh, sorry," I said.

I got back to weeding.

He turned away, shaking his head.

When I left his house that day, I saw the broken boxes from the hive I had smashed, sitting on top of his garbage can. I took them. Mrs. Biel must have thought I was stealing them. She gave me a mean look when I passed her house. But they were garbage. She couldn't call the cops on me for taking trash.

6

When I got home, I took the broken hive boxes out to my dad's wood shop. He had a big shed filled with tools. When he was alive, he'd been a carpenter. He'd taught me how to use all his tools. Sometimes I'd helped him.

He'd made chairs, tables, dressers. He'd made cabinets. And he'd made boxes. Big boxes and little boxes.

His shop was still just as he had left it. Everything put away. Everything neat and organized. As if he would come back any minute to use it again.

I put the broken beehive on the workbench. It was basically just a set of boxes. Boxes were easy. I knew how to make boxes.

When I'd been real young and cried at night, my dad used to take me out to his workshop so Mom could sleep. I'd loved to keep him company while he worked. He would give me things to play with, and I would stop crying and fall asleep holding them.

The first thing I ever remember is playing with his level. The level is a tool that has a space with a bubble in it. When you build a house, or a doorway, or a wood shed, you want it to be straight and perfect. The level shows you if you're building it right. You lay the level down on whatever you're building. If you're doing a good job, the bubble will be in the middle.

One day, when I was six or seven, we'd been in the wood shop and I had been playing with his level. I'd put it on the floor: flat and perfect. On the workbench: perfect. Then I'd put it on his head. The bubble had rolled to one side and the level had fallen off.

He'd laughed. "I guess I'm not level-headed," he'd said.

I knew what level-headed was. It meant calm and smart. He had been the most level-headed person I'd ever known.

He'd sat down, and I'd gone and leaned on his shoulder. He'd felt warm and strong.

He'd put down the piece of wood he was sanding and said, "Hey, Jacob, you want to know something cool? That bubble tells you something cosmic. You know what cosmic is? It means huge. As big as all of space." And he'd added, "That little level tells you how to find the Center of the Earth!"

"How?" I'd asked.

He'd held out the level. The bubble was exactly in the middle.

"If you could draw a line straight down from that bubble and kept going, you would hit the exact center of the earth."

That seemed magical to me. I'd taken the level and lined it up. Then imagined going straight down. Through the earth, straight down to the middle. It had almost been like I could feel the earth turning, with all the stars spread out around it.

My dad had been like that. He could take little things and make them seem big. He'd made everything interesting.

But now, ever since he died last year, nothing was interesting.

I sat on my dad's bench and looked at my empty hands. When my dad was alive, I didn't do stupid things.

We didn't have all these problems with money.

When my dad was alive, my mom was happy.

When my dad was alive, I was happy.

We'd had food in the fridge and cable on the TV. We never worried about losing our house. But it wasn't just that. We'd had a family. I had Dad and I could talk to him. Now it was just me and Mom. She worked so much that I hardly ever saw her. And when I did, I couldn't talk to her. And I kept doing stupid things. *Would I ever stop?*

Dad, I thought, *I wish you were here. I wish you could hear me. I wish I could talk to you.*

I looked around the room. He'd been halfway through making a dresser for my mom. On his workbench was a piece of paper where he had written down all the lengths of the wood that he needed. He had most of the dresser built.

All that was left was the drawers. It was beautiful. Cherry wood, smooth, and perfect.

I felt like any minute, he would walk in. Like he had never died. Never had cancer, never been sick. Just on a trip. He would walk in and pat me on the shoulder and say, "OK, Buddy, let's get to work. Could you measure this for me?"

I sat there a long time, but he never came. It got dark, and I kept sitting there.

Outside on the road, cars passed. Their headlights made long stripes of light that shone through the window and moved across the wall. Outside, people were going places. But inside the shed, nothing changed. My dad was still gone.

7

"Mow the lawn," the Bee Man said.

He had one of those old-timey lawn mowers that doesn't have a motor. You push it, and the blades spin around and cut the grass.

I spent the day shoving that mower around, mowing all the paths in between his hives. Whenever a bee flew close to me, I would duck. Like every few seconds. I could hear him laughing every time I jumped.

It was a fun day for him! Not as fun for me.

* * *

The next day, the Bee Man had a big smile on his face.

"For you," he said. He handed me a pile of rumpled-up white cloth.

"You want me to do your laundry?" I asked.

This was too much. Lawn work was one thing, but I was not about to wash his clothes.

He laughed. He slapped a hat like his hat on my head. It had a veil on it, just like his.

"What is this?" I asked.

"Today, you're going to start working the bees. Did you think you could do yard work forever? The hedge is cut. The yard is mowed. The weeds are pulled. The trash is gone. Now it's time for bees."

He took the pile of clothes away from me and shook it out to show me. It was an outfit of white coveralls. Just like his.

"But I'll get stung!"

He laughed. "Young man, do you know how many times I've been stung? Hundreds. It doesn't even hurt any more."

I said, "Well, it hurts me. And I don't like it."

He motioned with his hand. "Get dressed."

I put on the bee clothes. They were big and baggy. They smelled like smoke. The hat was too big for me. It was hard to see through the veil.

He said, "I'm giving you gloves. You don't really need them."

I was not about to play with bees with my bare hands. I put on the gloves.

It felt like getting suited up for war.

8

My heart was pounding. My leg still hurt from being stung the other day. I was still walking crooked.

We went over to one of the hives. The Bee Man got out his little metal teapot.

"This is a smoker," he said. "Bees talk to each other with smells. When you put smoke into a hive, the bees can't smell each other. They can't tell each other to sting you. Also, they eat a lot of honey when they smell smoke. They get so busy eating honey that they leave you alone. Most of the time." He laughed his little laugh.

I didn't think it was so funny.

He put leaves, grass, and sticks into the smoker and lit it with a match. When the fire was going, he closed the top. He pressed a flap on the side of the smoker. Clouds of smoke floated out of the spout.

He handed it to me. "OK, you make some smoke."

I pressed the flap and smoke came out.

He lifted the lid of the hive. Under it was a flat piece of wood with a hole in the middle.

"Puff some smoke right in there," he said. "Not much, just a little."

I pumped the smoker and aimed the smoke at the hole.

We waited.

"OK, let's open it up," he said.

He lifted the lid. I saw the frames hanging inside the hive. All of them were covered with bees. Some bees flew up, but they didn't seem angry.

"Give them a little smoke," he said. "A few gentle puffs." He took the smoker and showed me how.

"How many bees are in there?" I asked.

"About sixty thousand," he said.

"Sixty THOUSAND?" I backed away.

"These frames are all filled with honey."

He held one up. It looked like solid sunlight. He slid it back in, then picked up the whole box and took it off the stack. Then he took off another box and pointed at the box on the bottom of the stack.

"In this bottom box, you will find the queen bee."

"Is there a king bee?" I had always wondered about that.

"No, just a queen. Every bee in this hive is her daughter. Almost all of them. There might be a few boys. Her sons. But every bee you see working on a flower is a girl. Boy bees don't live long. They don't do any work. They just sit around the hive doing nothing. Sometimes they mate with a queen bee so she can lay eggs. Then they die. The ones that are still alive in fall get kicked out of the hive by all the girl bees. They're just extra mouths to feed and they're useless to the hive in winter time."

Some life, I thought.

He was lifting frames and looking carefully at them. "Here she is."

He pointed at a bee. I don't know how he found it in the crowd of 60,000 other bees, but he did. It was much bigger than any of the other bees.

"When you threw that rock at my hive, it broke open and the queen was lost. Maybe she was killed. Maybe she flew away. But when the queen dies, the hive will die. Unless they can get another queen."

"They just die? That's it?"

"That's it. They need a queen to keep laying eggs and making new bees. Sometimes, they can make a new queen from an egg that's in the hive. Other times, they can't. When that happens, the hive will die."

"Why do they die?"

"Each bee only lives a few weeks. Without the queen, there are no new bees to replace the ones that die. Also, the queen makes a special smell. That smell keeps the bees happy. If they don't smell the queen, the bees get confused and stop working. No work, no food, no life."

I leaned over and sniffed. The hive smelled sweet and lemony.

"Lemon furniture polish?"

"That smell is made by all the bees. It's the smell of a happy hive."

I looked at all the bees around the queen. They were feeding her and following her around. She was laying eggs. One tiny egg in each little cup of the hive.

"Those other bees, those are all the workers. All girls. They take care of the queen, they take care of the eggs. They collect nectar, the sweet juices from flowers. See that yellow dust on the bees? That's called pollen. They eat it. They collect that from flowers too."

Bees were crawling all over me. They were buzzing angrily at my veil.

9

"Listen," I said. "The bees. They're going to sting me."

He grabbed the smoker and puffed it at the bees, and on my clothes. The bees seemed to calm down.

"Bees will only sting you if they think you're going to hurt them, or hurt their hive. They don't sting you for fun."

"What about the one that stung me on the leg? It stung me over and over. I was just riding my bike."

"One bee stung you over and over? Is that why you're walking funny?"

"Yeah. I saw it. It stung me. Then it moved over and stung me again. It stung me three times."

"You saw it? It was the same insect?"

Was he stupid? I wondered. "Yes."

"That wasn't a bee."

"But I saw it!"

"Bees can only sting you once," he said. "After a honeybee stings you, it dies. The stinger rips out of its body and stays in your skin. That kills it. If something stung you more than once, it was a wasp. A lot of people can't tell the difference. They're both black and yellow, and they both sting. But wasps don't make honey. And wasps don't die when they sting. They can sting you over and over. And they will."

I was quiet. If a wasp is what stung me, then his bees had nothing to do with it. I had broken his hive for nothing.

10

When I got home, I looked in the fridge. Mom had been shopping. She must have gotten paid. There was a stack of frozen pizzas, more milk, some eggs, some cheese, apples, and some bread. And salad stuff. A feast.

I made a pizza, then went out to my dad's wood shop.

I picked up one of the Bee Man's broken boxes. I got the tape measure.

I measured the box, and wrote down the numbers I needed.

On shelves around the room, my dad had stacks of wood. He never threw out a piece of wood unless it was too small to use. There was plenty of wood. Some was fancy wood: cherry, maple, walnut, and others whose names I didn't know.

The Bee Man's hives were made of pine. I found some really nice pieces of pine and started cutting.

The hum of the saw really made me think of my dad.

He was the last one who touched these tools. Now, I was touching them. It was the closest to him that I could get. For the first time since he died, I felt just a little bit happy.

The wood felt good in my hands. It smelled good. I cut the parts of the box very carefully. I wanted it to be perfect. It took a long time. When I was done, I put it together with glue and nails. It was tight and even. A good job.

The shed smelled like fresh sawdust again. A good smell. A happy smell. It was the smell of my dad. He smelled like sawdust. He smelled like soap. He smelled like the oil he used to finish his furniture. When he came into the house after working in the wood shop, just smelling him made me feel happy. Like everything was OK because Dad was home.

So, I sort of knew how those bees felt. My dad was a man, not a queen bee, but without him, my mom and I just didn't know what to do.

Jacob and the Bee Man

11

The next morning, I took the new box with me.

"Where did you get this?" the Bee Man asked.

"I made it. It's to make up for the hive I broke. I'll make the rest of the hive, too. I took the broken pieces home so I could see how to make them."

He took it from me. Turned it over and looked at all the perfect little corners.

"Thank you, young man," he said.

That day he didn't work me as hard. He just showed me things. How the bees made rows and rows of perfect little cups to put the flower nectar in. How they packed pollen in some cups, and took care of baby bees in other ones. It was a whole world in there.

In the middle of the day, he brought out three jars of honey and a spoon. "Taste these," he said.

I did. I had never really had honey before. It tasted like flowers. A deep, rich, flowery flavor. The sweetness stayed on my tongue for a long time. It was one of the most delicious things I had ever eaten.

"At different times of the summer, the bees collect nectar from different flowers. That's why each jar tastes different from the others."

By the end of the day, I almost forgot to be afraid of the bees. He told me to pick up one of the frames and look at it. I kept my gloves on. But I did it. And it was an amazing, awesome feeling.

The next day, the phone rang at six in the morning. My mom was in the shower, so I got out of bed and answered it. *Who would call at six in the morning?*

It was the Bee Man.

"It's going to pour all day," he said. "Bees don't fly in the rain. They sit in the hive and they get mad. Stay home."

I had breakfast with my mom before she went to work at the dentist's office. It was the first meal I had eaten with her in a couple of weeks. Usually I didn't wake up until after she was gone. It felt like the old days, when we were happy.

I could tell she was happy, too. She made pancakes. We hadn't had pancakes since my dad died, either.

"So, how are things with Mr. Finley?" she asked.

"Good," I said. "He's kind of strange, but not bad."

After she went to work, I went out to the shop and spent the day in there, making the rest of his beehive. Two more boxes and some other parts that the boxes rested on. I also made the beehive cover with the little hole that you blow the smoke into.

It felt so good to be working with wood. I felt like my dad would be happy if he could see me. When I finished making the boxes and they were sitting so the glue could dry, I swept up the sawdust.

Then I dusted off the dresser he had been making for my mom. I found the notes my Dad had written about it. Little drawings of how he was going to make the drawers. And when I finished making the hive boxes, I found my dad's pile of cherry wood and started measuring out those drawers.

Drawers were just boxes, after all.

12

The next day was sunny.

The Bee Man must be so excited to have his servant back, I thought. I wondered what he would make me do today.

I took all the rest of the hive boxes and other parts over to his house. He had a big smile on his face when he saw them.

"You've been busy," he said.

I nodded.

"Did your dad teach you to build like that?"

"Yeah."

Another thing about small towns. Everyone knew about my dad.

"Beautiful work," he said. "He did beautiful work. And it looks like you got that skill from him."

"Thanks," I said.

We spent the day checking more of his hives. At every hive, he looked for the queen.

"It's OK if we can't find her," he said, "as long as we find some eggs. If you find eggs, you know she's in there making them."

He told me that you could tell if a hive was happy. He called it "queen right" by the way the bees were humming. They didn't hum the same way when the queen was gone.

It was hot under my veil, but I liked looking at the hives. I liked the bees. I liked seeing how they filled the frames with honey.

It was the first time I had been happy in a long time.

In the middle of the day, I had to use the bathroom.

"Go in the back door," he said. "Through the kitchen and down the hall. On the left."

His house was not like I thought it would be. I thought it would be creepy and dark and smell weird. A lonely, crazy old man's house. But it was more like a beehive. It smelled clean and lemony, and the rooms were painted yellow. Paintings of flowers hung on the walls.

In the hall, there were a lot of old photos of the same woman. Some were black and white. Others were in color. You could see the woman at every age in these photos.

First, she was young and beautiful. Then she was a little older and still looking good. Then my mom's age, and still pretty. And she was one of those people who are not just pretty, but you can tell they're nice. The kind of person you would want to talk to.

There were no pictures of her as an old woman. Did she die before she got old?

She must have been the Bee Man's wife, I thought. *And she died.*

He had loved her. He still loved her.

I wondered if he talked to her in his mind, like I did with my dad. I would bet that he did.

I went back outside. He looked different to me now. Before, he was just the Bee Man. Kind of like a cartoon person with his bee clothes and his veil, working his bees with his bare hands and telling me the stings didn't hurt him.

Now I could see his dark eyes behind his veil. It sounds weird, but now he was a real person to me. And I could see in his eyes that he knew about pain.

13

The next day, he had me set up the hive I had built. He gave me a bunch of empty frames to put in it. He showed me how to stack the parts.

After that, he told me to weed his gravel driveway. I did. Weeding was not my favorite thing to do, but it was OK.

It was boiling hot out. In the middle of the day, he said, "Come on in the kitchen. I have some lemonade."

His kitchen had a big, sunny window over the sink. When I washed my hands, I could still see all the beehives and flowers in the yard. Bees bumped lightly against the window as they worked on the flowers outside.

"Sit down." He waved his hand at the kitchen table. He put a plate of cheese sandwiches on the table. "Go ahead, eat."

I sat and ate.

He opened the refrigerator and took out a jug of lemonade. It was yellow, like his kitchen. It tasted different from other lemonade. More flowery.

"Sweetened with honey," he said.

We drank our lemonade. I could taste the flowers in it. He was quiet. He was one of those people who it was easy to be quiet with. This was a surprise to me. Most adults made me nervous.

It took me a long time to say it, but finally, I did. I took a deep breath. "I'm sorry about your bees."

"What bees?" he asked.

I said, "The ones in the hive I broke."

He nodded. "You rebuilt that beehive. I think we won't worry about those bees. I gave them a new home. And I gave them a new queen."

"Thanks."

He held up his glass of lemonade. "Cheers," he said.

I clinked my glass against his.

I never expected him to toast me with his glass like that, after what I did to his bees.

* * *

That night, I suddenly thought: *the Bee Man has his hive back. And the bees in it are OK. So does that mean I'm done working for him?*

You'd think I would be happy to be done. But I wasn't.

I liked it over there. Now, I was kind of afraid he would tell me to stop coming.

14

But the next morning, he didn't tell me we were done.

"I have news for you," he said. "Today, we're going to fill your new hive with bees."

I walked toward his backyard. I thought he had some extra bees back there.

"No, get in the truck."

"The truck? Where are we going?" *Now what?*

"We're going to get some bees!" He slapped his hands together. He was almost dancing with happiness. "This is one of the most fun things a beekeeper gets to do. Come on, let's go," he said.

"OK," I said.

I got into his beat-up old truck, but I kept my hand on the door handle, just in case I had to jump out. He looked over at me. I could tell he knew what I was thinking. He seemed to think it was funny.

We only drove a few blocks. He stopped at the car wash.

"This is it!" he said. He was really excited.

"We're going to wash the truck?" I asked.

I sat low in my seat, hoping the car wash owner wouldn't see me. Just a few days ago, he had told me what a dirtbag I was.

"No, we're going to get some bees!" the Bee Man said.

He pointed. In the parking lot of the car wash was a white car that was covered with bees. The car wash owner stood next to it, looking angry. A ball of bees was hanging off the bumper of the car. A ball of bees that was the size of a basketball.

"That's a swarm," the Bee Man said. "Bees do that when the hive grows and there are too many bees. The bees make a new queen in the hive. The new queen and a lot of the bees leave. They look for a new place to live. While they're looking, they stop and rest. Today, this swarm is resting on that car. And you're going to collect them."

"I'm going to collect them? Me? By myself?"

"I brought your bee clothes. Here, put them on."

A crowd of people was gathering around the car. Almost like a swarm of bees.

When we got out of the truck and started putting on our bee clothes, all the people moved back. The Bee Man had a roll of that yellow tape that says CAUTION CAUTION CAUTION on it, and some orange traffic cones. He used them to make a big circle around the car. The crowd of people made a solid wall around the circle of tape.

The owner of the car wash pushed through the crowd and stared at me. He stood with his arms folded and his legs apart, like he thought I was going to rob the place. Or burn it down.

"I thought I told you to get lost," he said to me. And he said to the Bee Man, "Hey, Cliff, what are you doing with this kid? I don't want him on my property."

I felt like just walking away. *Would people ever shut up about that?* I put on my veil so the car wash guy couldn't see my face. Then I went to the truck and stood next to it. Just in case the Bee Man told me we had to leave.

"He's my helper," the Bee Man said, "and if you want these bees out of here, you'll leave him alone. Let him work."

"OK, OK, get the bees out of here," the car wash guy said. He shook his head. He cursed under his breath.

The Bee Man came over to the truck. "Just ignore that guy," he said, jerking his head at the car wash owner. "He's the same age I am. He did plenty of bad things when we were young. I know all about him. And he knows I know."

He slapped his hands together. "Now, let's get back to the bees. Just do what I tell you to do. You're going to catch this swarm of bees. All by yourself."

15

The crowd pressed against the CAUTION tape. Everyone had their cellphones out, taking photos. The car wash guy went into his building and watched us from behind his big, glass window.

The Bee Man handed me a plastic spray bottle. He said, "This has sugar water in it. You spray it over the swarm. Don't soak them. Just do it lightly. It will keep them busy and calm them down."

I sprayed them with the sugar water.

"Now give them a little smoke." He handed me the smoker.

I puffed a little smoke at them.

"Now," he said, "we have to knock the bees off."

That sounded crazy to me. Knocking off a ball of bees? That seemed like a good way to get stung.

He went to the truck and got the boxes I had made. He also had a set of frames. He put frames into one of my boxes. Now it looked like a beehive.

He took out a little bottle. "This is lemongrass oil. It smells like a happy hive. Put a few drops of it on this tissue. Then put the tissue into the hive. That will make it smell like home to them."

I did. It had that nice lemon smell.

"Now put the hive next to the car."

I moved the hive over, so it was right under the bumper of the car.

"Now," the Bee Man said, "give them a little more sugar water. A little smoke. When I say 'Go,' use your gloves to knock that ball of bees off the car and onto the hive. Gently! The queen is in the middle of that ball of bees. If we get the queen into the hive, all the bees will follow her. OK, Go."

Slowly, I put my gloved hands over the ball of bees. My heart was pounding. Sweat was pouring down my face.

The bees did not seem to notice me. Some of them flew around, but they weren't trying to sting me. I gently pushed the ball of bees down and most of them fell onto the hive. They started crawling down into the spaces between the frames.

I knocked off more bees. It was an amazing feeling. I was picking up gobs of bees in my hands and dropping them onto the hive, and they weren't stinging me!

The crowd clapped and cheered. I felt awesome!

The Bee Man said, "It looks like you got the queen. See how the ones that were flying around are going into the hive? They're following the queen. She's in there. They'll go wherever she goes. Now we wait for the rest of them to come."

We sat on the ground in the hot parking lot and waited. After a while, most of the bees that were flying around went into the hive. Just like the bees, the people in the crowd got into their cars and drove away. The car wash guy was still hiding inside.

"OK," the Bee Man said. "Nice work. I think this calls for a lemonade."

He picked up the hive, set it in the back of his truck, and strapped it down.

16

Back at his house, in his yellow kitchen, we toasted each other again. I could see the new hive out his kitchen window.

"That hive is yours, now," the Bee Man said.

"No, it's yours. I made it for you because I broke your other one."

"I'm telling you, it's yours. You built the hive, you caught the swarm. You can keep it here. Come over and learn to work it. I'll keep an eye on it for you when you're busy."

I just stared at him. I couldn't believe this. *Why was he doing this for me?* I wondered.

He looked right at me. "Jacob, this is a small town. People talk. I know what you did last year."

I sighed. Now, he would tell me how much of a jerk he thought I was.

He took a sip of lemonade and looked at the flower pictures on his walls. And instead of talking about last year, he said, "Let me tell you something about bees. Bees do a million little things. Each little thing seems like nothing. They get one tiny drink of flower nectar. Or one speck of pollen. But after a while, these things add up. Do you know how many bees it takes to make one teaspoon of honey?"

I said nothing. I had no idea.

"Twelve bees spend their whole lives working to make one teaspoon of honey. It takes two million visits to flowers to make a pound of honey. Can you imagine doing anything two million times? Bees do. And a good hive can make over two hundred pounds of honey."

I looked at the bottle of honey on the table between us. Two million flowers.

He looked out the window at the sky. "I was married to the most wonderful woman. The bees were her idea. She loved flowers and she loved bees. But she died young. When she got sick, she told me, 'Even if I die, you have to keep going. Keep working. Be like a bee, no matter what. Even if you think you're doing nothing. Even if you think your work is really small and doesn't mean anything. Little things mean a lot.'"

He took a sip of lemonade. Then he said, "Jacob, when you made me a new box, that was a little thing. But it meant a lot."

I nodded.

"You may not believe this, but I was a kid, once. I know all about the things kids do. I don't care what you did last year. It's over. I care about what you're doing now. I knew you'd be a good beekeeper when I saw you watching the bees. When you stopped weeding and just watched them. You were interested. I saw it in your face. Keep your hive here. If you get another job, that's fine. You can come over when you have time and I'll still teach you how to work with the bees. If you don't get a summer job, build some more hives. I know every beekeeper in this state. They all need new hives. You can sell every hive you can make. If you make them from fancy wood, you can sell them for more money. There are plenty of city people who would pay a lot of money for a hive made of cherry, or walnut, or some other nice wood."

* * *

When I got home, Mom wasn't there. I would wait up for her, so I could tell her. I had a job! Not a job I ever thought I would have. *A beekeeper? Or a carpenter? Or both?*

I went out to the shed. My dad's notes were on the workbench, where I had left them. All his measurements for my mom's dresser. I would finish that first. Then I would make more hives.

I sat down, closed my eyes, and leaned my head back. I let out a deep breath.

All the past year of being called names and having people look at me like I was a criminal. I could feel it sliding off me.

It might never go away. People might not forget.

But maybe they would. In time.

"It's over," I said out loud, just like the Bee Man said at his kitchen table. "Over."

And then I picked up a piece of cherry wood and a pencil and a tape measure, and I got to work.

About The Author

Kelly Winters is a part-time writer and a full-time mom. She homeschools her son, who struggles with reading comprehension, so contributing a story to the first Story Share contest was important to her! She is honored to be a part of any endeavor that helps kids become more interested and able readers.

About The Publisher

Story Shares is a nonprofit focused on supporting the millions of teens and adults who struggle with reading by creating a new shelf in the library specifically for them. The ever-growing collection features content that is compelling and culturally relevant for teens and adults, yet still readable at a range of lower reading levels.

Story Shares generates content by engaging deeply with writers, bringing together a community to create this new kind of book. With more intriguing and approachable stories to choose from, the teens and adults who have fallen behind are improving their skills and beginning to discover the joy of reading. For more information, visit storyshares.org.

Easy to Read. Hard to Put Down.